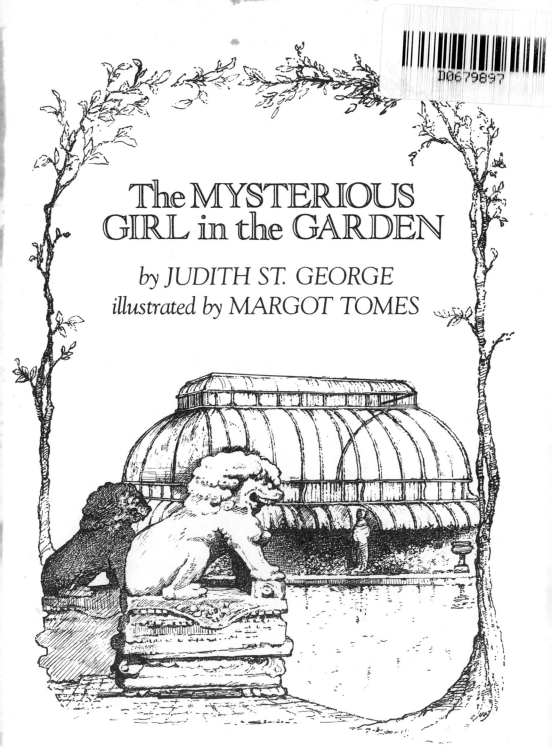

The MYSTERIOUS GIRL in the GARDEN

by JUDITH ST. GEORGE
illustrated by MARGOT TOMES

G.P. PUTNAM'S SONS · NEW YORK

COPY 6

Text copyright © 1981 by Judith St. George
Illustrations copyright © 1981 by Margot Tomes
All rights reserved. Published simultaneously in
Canada by Academic Press Canada Limited, Toronto.
Printed in the United States of America
First Impression
Library of Congress Cataloging in Publication Data
St. George, Judith,
The mysterious girl in the garden.
Summary: During daily visits to Kew Gardens
a ten-year-old American girl finds herself
transported back to Kew Palace in 1805 where
she meets Princess Charlotte Augusta, future
queen of England.
[1. England—Fiction.   2. Princesses—
Fiction.   3. Space and time—Fiction]
I. Tomes, Margot.   II. Title.
PZ7.S142Mx   [Fic]   81-5931
ISBN 0-399-20822-4   AACR2

For Connie and Bill

CHAPTER   1

"Mom, we're not going to Kew Gardens again to-day, are we?" Terrie poured more milk on her cereal than she needed and it splashed on the table.

"Please don't start that again, Terrie. You know I'll be working at Kew Gardens all summer," her mother answered. She seemed annoyed about the milk, but she mopped it up without a word.

Terrie Wright and her parents were spending the summer in Chiswick, England, just outside of London. Mr. Wright had to be in England on business and Mrs. Wright had decided to take courses at the Kew Botanic Gardens nearby. That meant Terrie had to hang around the Gardens every day with nothing to do. The worst part was she could have spent the summer with her grandmother on Cape Cod. Granny had a house right on the beach and she had invited not only Terrie but her dog, Wags, too. Terrie had begged and nagged and pleaded with her parents to let her go. But they had said no, she had to come to England with them. So here she was, having the most boring, awful summer an almost-eleven-year-old American girl ever had.

"I'll tell you what, Terrie. On Saturday we'll go to the London Zoo and have a Chinese dinner afterwards. How does that sound?" Dad reached across the table and squeezed Terrie's hand.

"Okay, I guess," Terrie mumbled. That still left almost the whole week to get through.

"When we're in London, let's get your hair cut, Terrie," Mom suggested. "It's much too long."

"I like it long."

Mrs. Wright didn't answer. Terrie figured she probably didn't want to argue. Mom must know what a terrible summer she was having, when she could have been swimming and sailing every day on Cape Cod.

Tuesday was Mrs. Wright's day to work in the Bamboo Garden out by the Queen's Cottage. Kew Botanic Gardens covered three hundred acres and it was a long walk. Neither Terrie nor her mother said much the whole way. Mrs. Wright was glancing through her notes and Terrie was wondering what she would do all day. When they arrived at the Queen's Cottage, Terrie flopped down on a park bench. She had already been through the Cottage and it was a big nothing, just a house with a thatched roof that some queen had built two

hundred years ago.

"I've packed us a nice picnic lunch," Mrs. Wright said. "I'll come back at noon and we can eat in the rose garden."

"Mmm."

Mrs. Wright had already started to leave, but now she turned back. "Really, Terrie, I wish you weren't so negative. I know this summer isn't very exciting for you, but you've closed your mind to enjoying yourself in any way. I saw a whole group of children sailing boats on the pond yesterday. Your father and I would be happy to buy you a boat so you can join them."

"Babies sail boats, Mom. I'm not a baby."

"Well, sometimes you act like one." Mom handed Terrie her tote bag. "There's plenty in here to keep you busy. Good-bye, dear." She gave Terrie a worried kind of kiss and left.

Terrie didn't even open her tote bag. She already knew what was in it—books to read, her flute to practice, playing cards and writing paper. Boring, boring, boring. Terrie watched two old ladies feeding pigeons. They looked bored too. Finally, clucking and cooing like pigeons themselves, they got up and walked away.

Terrie was still slumped on the bench doing nothing when she saw the dog. He was a small, white dog with long hair that covered his eyes. He was chasing a red ball that rolled over the grass. A little bell around his neck tinkled. He picked up the ball in his mouth, then trotted into an enormous stand of rhododendron bushes. Because Terrie knew dogs weren't allowed in Kew Gardens, she tried to watch where he went. But she couldn't see into the dense rhododendrons, which were at least twice as high as a tall man. The ball flew out again. It bounced over the grass and stopped by her foot. A moment later, the little dog ran out after it.

Terrie had never liked long-haired dogs much,

but she missed Wags terribly. And this dog was cute. He had a prancing kind of walk as if he were on the most important errand in the world. Without even looking at Terrie, he picked up the ball and strutted back into the bushes with it.

Terrie stood up, walked over to the rhododendrons, and peered in. But she couldn't see anything more than twisted roots, thick branches and big shiny leaves.

Swish, out came the ball again, followed by the white dog with his jingling bell. He brushed so close Terrie could have touched him. This time she went after him. She stooped under a low hanging branch and entered the shadowy thicket. Two steps farther in and the leaves became a dark roof. Even the air seemed cooler and damper. Ahead of her, Terrie saw the flash of a white tail. She stumbled after it in the dim light.

"For pity's sake, can't I be left alone for five minutes? Truly, I shall expire of impatience."

Terrie was so surprised she jumped back, cracking her shoulder on a branch. She rubbed her shoulder where it hurt and looked in the direction

of the voice. A girl about her age sat on a dusty root, her feet tucked up under her long skirts. The little dog played with his ball nearby.

The girl seemed furious as she glared at Terrie. "What do they want of me this time?" she demanded. "I promised I wouldn't stray. Still, they send their spies to snoop on me. Give me your message, girl, and begone."

Terrie cleared her throat to answer, but nothing came out. She could only stare.

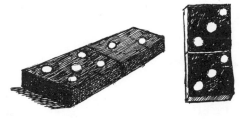

CHAPTER 2

"Must I repeat myself? What do they want of me now?" the girl asked even more crossly than before.

Terrie was getting cross herself. "No one wants you for anything. I saw your dog and followed him in here, that's all."

The girl reached down and rubbed her dog's ears. "Lioni is my dog. He does anything I tell him. He will even attack you if I give the order." The girl stuck her chin up in the air.

Lioni didn't look like he would attack anyone. Besides, Terrie had always gotten along well with dogs. She crouched down and whistled. "Here, Lioni, here, boy."

The dog got up and padded right over. Terrie scratched his throat as he wagged his tail with pleasure.

The girl jammed her hands on her hips. "I don't believe it. Lioni is my dog and mine alone. He hates everyone else."

Terrie had to laugh as Lioni nuzzled into her lap. "He doesn't hate me." Never in her life had she met such an impossible girl. And her outfit was unbelievable. She wore earrings, a necklace, bracelets, and a long dress that looked like a nightgown. Maybe it *was* a nightgown and she was sleepwalking.

"Humph." The girl scowled, her hands still on her hips. "This is my private place. You have no right to be here. I order you to leave."

Terrie smiled, hoping it would annoy her. "I have as much right to be here as you do."

"You certainly do not. My grandfather owns all this land. I shall call for my guards if you don't leave."

"Will they attack me like your dog did?"

The girl sputtered. "How dare you be flippant with me, Princess Charlotte Augusta of Windsor Castle, Carlton House and Kew Palace, future queen of England?"

Terrie stood up and curtsied. "Pardon me for not introducing myself, Your Majesty. I am Princess Terrie Ann Wright of Stilton, Massachusetts, future president of the United States."

"United States!" the girl cried. "I should have guessed from your horrid accent that you were American. Who would expect anything more from an American female than to have a man's name and to appear before me in trousers?"

"Now just a minute . . ."

The girl Charlotte made a big show of looking at the watch pinned to her dress as if the conversation bored her. "Personally I never believed that losing the American colonies was the tragedy that Grandpapa thought it was. A country full of ragtag failures never was worth fighting a war over."

That was too much. Terrie leaped up, ready to take Charlotte on. But a yelp of pain stopped her. She had jumped on Lioni's foot. He whimpered and hobbled back to his mistress.

The girl hugged her injured dog. "Did that dreadful person harm you, my precious?"

Terrie patted him too. "I'm sorry. I didn't mean to hurt him."

"Princess Charlotte, where are you? Are you sulking in those bushes again?"

It was a woman's shrill voice right outside the rhododendron bushes. Charlotte put her finger to her lips for Terrie to be still. "I'm here, Miss Hayman," she called back, all nicey-nice. She shook Lioni's bell so it jingled. "Hear? Lioni's with me. He hurt his paw and I am comforting him."

"You mustn't frighten me. I feared something had happened to you."

"Who . . . ?" Terrie started to ask, but Charlotte shook her head for silence.

"That was Miss Hayman, my great goose of a governess," Charlotte whispered after a few minutes. "She never lets me be. If she doesn't see Lioni or hear his bell, she pursues me."

Terrie stared at Charlotte. What was going on? Charlotte had said she was a princess and that woman had called her princess too. They must both be crazy. Terrie jumped up and brushed off her jeans. "I'd better go," she announced.

"No, please don't." All of a sudden, Charlotte didn't sound so uppity. "I mean, I have nothing to entertain me. I haven't seen anyone my own age since I arrived here at Kew Palace in June to spend the summer with my grandparents."

Terrie could understand that. She hadn't had anything to do since she arrived in June either. Besides, Charlotte didn't really seem dangerous and her dog Lioni was adorable. He had dropped his ball in Terrie's lap for her to play with him. "I'll stay only if you stop ordering me around," Terrie agreed.

"I order anyone around I please." Charlotte's chin went up in the air again. Then she seemed to wilt. "At least I order my guards around. Otherwise, everyone orders me about, Papa and Grandmama and Grandpapa and all my aunts and uncles. I'm like a piece of taffy pulled first in one direction, then in another."

For some reason, Terrie felt sorry for her. "I get ordered around too," she said. "I wanted to stay with my grandmother this summer, but my mother and father ordered me to come here to England with them. It's been the worst summer I ever had." Terrie picked up the ball and threw it out of the bushes. Lioni took off after it. His injured paw seemed all better.

"If my parents did anything together, I would be pleased beyond measure." Charlotte scratched lines in the hard dirt with the toe of her black slipper. "Mama and Papa have been separated since seventeen ninety-six. They have hardly spoken to each other since the year I was born."

Seventeen ninety-six! Charlotte *was* crazy. "Are your parents divorced?" Maybe that was why Charlotte was so weird.

"Naturally not. My father is the Prince of Wales

and royalty never divorce. But Mama and Papa detest each other and it has caused great gossip and scandal."

Lioni had already returned, and without thinking, Terrie took the ball from his mouth and tossed it out of the bushes again.

"Because Papa won't let me live with Mama, I had nowhere to go this summer," Charlotte went on. "That's why I'm here at Kew Palace with my grandparents, King George III and Queen Charlotte. It's been horrid. My parents have always fought over me, but now my grandparents have joined in the bickering. And Grandpapa's court is dull beyond words. Even his subjects call him 'Farmer George.' When I become queen, my court will sparkle with wit and gay music and interesting people."

Wow, it was time to get off the subject of parents, Terrie decided. She pointed to a big hatbox half-hidden behind a root. "What's that?" she asked.

"It's my playbox." Charlotte pulled out the box. It was covered with colored, varnished paper with "Royal Playthings" stenciled on the top. She lifted the cover. Inside were two packs of playing cards, a tiny chess set, a backgammon board and a set of dominoes.

"I always win at dominoes," Charlotte declared. "Are you willing to risk a game with me?"

Terrie had never met anyone in her life who could be pathetic one minute and completely obnoxious the next. "You bet I am," Terrie answered, "and you'd better watch out. I'm the best domino player in Stilton, Massachusetts."

CHAPTER 3

Terrie had a surprisingly good time with Charlotte. They each won two games of dominoes and Terrie was all set for a rematch the next day. But when she woke up, she saw it was raining. It wasn't just raining, it was pouring. There would be no finding Charlotte in the park today. And rainy days in Kew Gardens were deadly. Mrs. Wright always worked in the greenhouse, which Terrie hated because it was so hot and steamy.

But as Terrie and her mother hurried through the rain from the main gate to the greenhouse, Terrie noticed the Kew Palace building set back a way from the path. She remembered that was where Charlotte had said she was spending her summer. Terrie knew that was impossible because Kew Palace was a museum, but all of a sudden, taking a tour through the palace seemed like a good idea. Mrs. Wright, delighted at Terrie's new interest in history, was happy to buy her a ticket.

Terrie took her time walking through the building. It wasn't big, more of a house than a palace, but every room had a fireplace and great high windows that let in lots of light. Deep window seats in the King's Breakfast Room were perfect for snuggling up with a book. Terrie looked out one of the rear windows. A lovely formal garden bloomed out back, all soft heathery blues and silvers and purples in the rain. The highest point in the garden was a gazebo that overlooked the River Thames as it slowly flowed toward London.

The museum display was in the last room of the palace. Terrie and a guard sitting on a stool reading his newspaper were the only ones in the room. Terrie strolled around looking at everything and reading her booklet. King George III and Queen Charlotte had first stayed at Kew Palace in 1760 and lived here on and off for fifty years. There were portraits of them both, as well as pictures of their fifteen children. Fifteen children. It seemed like an awful lot. As Terrie studied the portraits, the words "Farmer George" caught her eye. Wasn't that what Charlotte had called her grandfather?

From then on, Terrie paid closer attention to the displays and the descriptions that went with them. Then unexpectedly, she found herself reading about Princess Charlotte Augusta. As the only child of King George III's oldest son, she was the future queen of England. Princess Charlotte's parents separated soon after her birth and for years Charlotte was shuttled back and forth between her parents and grandparents.

It was just the way Charlotte had described herself. But that was ridiculous. That girl in the rhododendron bushes couldn't be Princess Charlotte Augusta. Then Terrie almost laughed out loud. Charlotte must have toured Kew Palace too, read all this history and made up a big fat story. And it had been a pretty good story, Terrie had to admit.

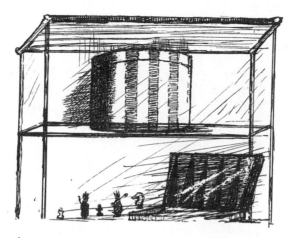

The glass case of toys was the last display in the room. Terrie glanced at it in passing, then stopped short. A colored, varnished hatbox with "Royal Playthings" lettered across the top sat in the middle of the case. Surrounding it were two packs of faded playing cards, a tiny chess set, a backgammon game and a yellowed set of ivory dominoes.

As Terrie raised her eyes to a picture above the case, little mice feet scampered up her back. She was looking at a portrait of a young girl about her own age with short blonde hair. The girl wore a necklace, bracelets, earrings and a dress that looked like a nightgown with a tiny watch pinned to it. And in her lap was a little dog with long white hair. Terrie stared at the girl's bright blue eyes set in a mischievous face, and the bright blue eyes seemed to stare back at her. "Princess Charlotte Augusta and her Maltese terrier, Lioni. 1805," stated the label.

Terrie jumped as a loud harrumph sounded behind her. It was only the guard clearing his throat
and rattling his newspaper. Before Terrie's heart
had been ready to burst through her shirt, now it
didn't seem to be beating at all. Terrie turned back
to the portrait. Princess Charlotte Augusta was the
same in every way as the girl Terrie had met, and
there was the toybox . . . and Lioni . . . and Charlotte's story about her parents . . .

Stop it, Terrie told herself, it can't be. It's just
an English girl playing dress-up to fool a dumb
American. Yes, it was only a joke. Nevertheless,
Terrie stood looking at Princess Charlotte's portrait for a long, long time.

CHAPTER   4

Terrie couldn't wait to get to Kew Gardens the next day to find Charlotte. She planned to play along, then POW, let Charlotte know she was onto her game. No English girl was going to put something over on her.

"It certainly is nice to see you cheerful for a change," Mrs. Wright said as she and Terrie made their way through the main gate. "I knew you'd have fun if you just gave yourself a chance."

"I'm going out to the Queen's Cottage," Terrie told her. "I'll meet you for lunch."

Her mother gave her a kiss. "Love you, Terrie."

"Love you, too, Mom."

Terrie ran through the wet grass all the way to the Queen's Cottage. By the time she reached the rhododendron bushes, her sneakers were soaked. The broad leaves sprinkled down a shower of drops as she slipped through the narrow entrance.

"Charlotte, where are you? Lioni?" Terrie tried

to keep the laughter out of her voice.

The maze of rhododendron roots and trunks was confusing, and Terrie searched through them a long time before she realized that Charlotte was nowhere about. Not anywhere. Terrie was surprised at how disappointed she felt. And it wasn't just that now she had to spend the day alone. Charlotte presented a challenge that she had looked forward to.

The next day Terrie dragged her feet. Without Charlotte, it was back to the same old boring Kew Gardens routine. "Mom, there is absolutely nothing to do in that whole place. Can't I stay home today and watch TV?"

"No, Terrie, I'm sorry. I'd worry about you alone in the apartment. Besides, if only you'd make a little effort, I'm sure you'd meet other children. What about that group that sails boats on the pond?"

"They won't speak to me." That was only partly true. A red-headed girl had acted friendly and asked Terrie if she were an American. Terrie had said yes, then walked on. They had all looked younger than she.

Mrs. Wright sighed. "Then practice your flute, Terrie. Otherwise you'll forget everything you've learned."

It turned out to be the most boring week yet. Terrie wrote eight letters, read three books and in desperation even practiced her flute. Though she began every day by searching for Charlotte and Lioni in the rhododendron bushes out by the Queen's Cottage, she never found them.

At last it was Friday. Weekends weren't so bad. On weekends, Terrie and her parents took boat trips or watched a polo game in the park or went to the movies. Still, Terrie had all of Friday ahead of her. She decided to spend the morning in the gazebo behind Kew Palace. From there she could watch the boats on the River Thames beyond the high brick wall.

Terrie arrived early. She and a workman were the only ones in the garden. During the past week, all the roses had bloomed, creamy white and yellow and peach and scarlet. Shivery cobwebs stretched from one blossom to another. The fountain splashed cheerfully and two fat English robins were busy scratching for breakfast.

Terrie settled down on the gazebo bench. She had planned to write a letter to her grandmother, but something about the peaceful, quiet garden made her pick up her flute instead. She turned to face the river as she played. Running water and flute music just naturally belonged together.

"Woorf. Woorf."

A little dog with long hair over his eyes darted out from behind a bed of crimson roses. He ran down the path, scooted around a holly hedge and disappeared.

Terrie dropped her flute on the bench and took off after him. As she turned the corner by the holly hedge, the little dog was just ahead of her. Then he took a right turn and was gone. Terrie skidded on the loose gravel of the path as she ran after him. There he was. It was Lioni. And with him was Charlotte, seated on a bench with a needlework sampler in her lap. Her blonde eyebrows pulled together in an angry line when she saw Terrie.

"For pity's sake, where have you been?" she demanded. "I've been waiting for you all week."

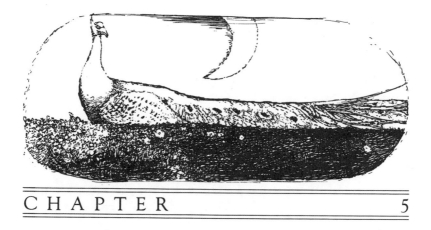

CHAPTER 5

Lioni barked a greeting as Terrie leaned down to pat him. It saved her from having to look at Charlotte or come up with anything to say.

"I thought you said you came to Kew every day. Where have you been?" Charlotte demanded again.

While Lioni danced happy little circles around her, Terrie glanced at Charlotte. Charlotte's blue eyes, her short blonde hair, her dress, her jewelry, were all identical to the portrait in the museum. Not similar. Identical. With that realization, Terrie knew it wasn't a joke or a game or a put-on. This was Princess Charlotte Augusta and her Maltese terrier Lioni. Terrie took a startled step backwards, too stunned to answer.

"I assumed you had sailed back to America." Charlotte picked up her needlework and started stitching with a bright green thread.

What Terrie wanted at that moment was to get

out of there. But she couldn't. Her knees had locked. "I . . . I . . . looked for you every day at the Queen's Cot . . . Cottage . . ." she stammered.

"I'm only there on Tuesdays when Grandmama picnics with her ladies-in-waiting. Otherwise I'm here at Kew Palace, forever and ever here."

Without warning, Terrie's knees unlocked and she sank down on the opposite end of the bench from Charlotte. She touched the wooden seat. It was real. The sharp gravel under her sneakers was real. Lioni licking her fingers was warmly real too. Everything was real. And yet unreal. As Terrie groped for something to say, to do, to connect her with the familiar, she noticed a flute lying on the bench. She picked it up. "Is this yours?" she asked.

"No, it's not mine. It's Lioni's." Charlotte reached over and took the flute away from Terrie.

It was the answer Terrie needed. It was impossible to make up anyone so disagreeable. Terrie watched as Charlotte put the flute to her lips and played a simple melody. Though Terrie didn't know the tune, she knew Charlotte didn't play very well. Somehow that made her feel better.

"I play the flute too," Terrie said. "I'll go get mine."

Terrie ducked around the holly hedge and ran up the gazebo path. She had already picked up her flute and started back down when she stopped.

The formal garden behind Kew Palace looked the same and yet not the same. There were no workmen or gardeners or people strolling around. Only a few peacocks strutted along the garden paths and two men in strange costumes were pruning trees. But they weren't in costume, Terrie realized, they were gardeners, King George III's gardeners, seeing to their work in the year 1805. Impossible. Terrie stood a moment as one of the peacocks promenaded past her. A beautiful bright blue feather fell at her feet. Without thinking, Terrie picked it up and put it in her pocket before slowly heading back to where Charlotte waited.

The flute was a help. It felt solid and familiar in Terrie's hands and when she raised it to her lips, the sound it made was familiar too. It linked her to everything she knew. But Charlotte must have thought her playing was funny. By the time Terrie finished, Charlotte was laughing.

"I thought you said you played the flute," Charlotte said.

Terrie knew she wasn't very good. "I've only been playing a year and a half," she explained.

Charlotte giggled. "So have I," she admitted.

The two girls smiled at each other and suddenly everything was all right between them. They both picked up their flutes. First Charlotte taught Terrie "Hearts of Oak," then Terrie taught Charlotte "Greensleeves." Lioni spent the time chasing butterflies in and out of the shrubbery. They had been playing for more than an hour when a man's voice shouted from somewhere beyond the holly hedge.

"Princess Charlotte, please come in for your Latin instruction."

"That's Reverend Mr. Notte," Charlotte explained in a whisper. She gathered up her needlework and flute and snapped her fingers for Lioni to follow. "Be certain to meet me here in the gar-

den on the morrow. I'll make plans for us," Charlotte directed, and she left without waiting for Terrie's reply.

Charlotte's bossiness was just too much. Then Terrie remembered. Charlotte had a right to be bossy. She was Princess Charlotte Augusta, future queen of England. But that couldn't be. Princess Charlotte Augusta was born almost two hundred years ago, the daughter of the Prince of Wales and granddaughter of King George III. And Terrie knew from her American history that King George III had been king during the American Revolution.

As Terrie sank back on the bench in total confusion, she noticed a green thread caught on a twig. She leaned over and plucked it off. It was the same color thread that Charlotte had been sewing with. As Terrie tucked the thread in her jeans' pocket along with the peacock feather, she realized it *was* possible that her friend Charlotte and Princess Charlotte Augusta were one and the same. It was not only possible, it was a certainty. And the knowledge was a warm, glowing secret inside her.

CHAPTER _____ 6

As soon as Terrie left her mother the next morning, she ran into the Kew Palace garden and up to the gazebo. Charlotte had said something about making plans for the day, and Terrie couldn't wait. She had only been there a few minutes when she heard Lioni's sharp little bark and saw him at the bottom of the gazebo path as if he were waiting for her. Sure enough, just like the day before, Lioni led her straight to Charlotte.

Charlotte's blue eyes sparkled with excitement. "Everyone in the palace has gone to some dull affair," she announced. "Only old Cook is here to watch me and she never leaves her room. We can play in the palace all morning."

Everyone was gone. It sounded safe enough. Nevertheless, Terrie's heart was somewhere in her throat as she followed Charlotte up the back palace stairs.

Charlotte saw her hesitate. "I told you no one

is here, Terrie. Come, I want to show you my bedchamber."

Charlotte's bedroom, on the third floor of the palace, was like a treetop eagle's nest overlooking Kew Gardens. Only it wasn't the Kew Gardens that Terrie knew. When she poked her head out the open window, she was startled to see no mothers pushing baby carriages or teenagers playing Frisbee or old people sitting on blankets eating picnic lunches. Instead all she saw were a couple of dozen sheep munching on the sweeping front lawn and five or six grazing cows over by a barn. Terrie quickly pulled in her head. She was better off not thinking too much about where she was or what she was doing.

Behind her Charlotte had opened the doors to her big Dutch wardrobe. "We can play dress-up."

The sight of Charlotte's beautiful clothes made Terrie feel better. They were in all the soft colors of a Kew Gardens rose bed.

"May I try one on?" she breathed.

"Of course. And I would like to dress in your strange garments."

Terrie tossed her clothes on the bed for Charlotte, and selected a creamy silk dress sewn with tiny pink flowers. While Terrie slipped the gown over her head, Charlotte pulled on Terrie's jeans and sweater. She stared in bewilderment at the blue jeans' zipper.

Terrie laughed, reached over and zipped it up. Then the two of them paraded around Charlotte's room and up and down the hall waving ostrich feather fans. Then, while Charlotte ran and jumped and cavorted in the new-found freedom of blue jeans, Terrie tried on one after another of Charlotte's dresses. She saved the best for last, a blue silk gown trimmed with lace with a matching lace picture hat.

"That's my shepherdess costume for the masquerade ball next month. A mask and a shepherd's crook go with it. Would you like to try them on?" Charlotte asked.

What a foolish question. The silk dress slithered over Terrie's arms. Though it was a little tight and a little long, Terrie knew she must look beautiful in it. "Where is your mirror?" she asked.

"Do you mean a looking-glass? The only one in the palace is in Grandmama's bedchamber," Charlotte answered.

Leaving Lioni curled up asleep, the two girls hurried down the stairs to the second floor. Terrie's long skirts swished around her ankles and tickled her bare feet. By the time they reached the queen's bedchamber, she was sweeping along like royalty herself.

The queen's bedchamber was much larger than Charlotte's, with an enormous four-poster bed in the middle of it. Charlotte opened the queen's wardrobe and on the back of one of the doors was a long mirror. As Terrie admired herself in the blue shepherdess costume, she couldn't help noticing the queen's wardrobe—rows and rows of gowns that were even more beautiful than Charlotte's. On the upper shelf were feathered headpieces and tiaras and even wigs on stands. The sight of so much finery caught Terrie up short. She was in the queen's bedroom! She quickly shut the wardrobe doors and backed away.

"Maybe we should play outside, Charlotte," she suggested.

"Nonsense, I told you no one is home." Charlotte ran across the room and took a flying leap onto the queen's huge bed. She turned a somersault, then stood on her head. "Grandmama lies here in bed to receive her subjects. Perhaps if she wore trousers like yours she wouldn't be such a slug-a-bed." Charlotte laughed as she propped herself up on the pillows.

Terrie smothered a laugh as she made a deep curtsy. "Your Majesty is kind to receive such a humble servant as me."

"Come closer, over here." Charlotte beckoned to Terrie.

"Yes, Your Majesty, on bended knee." Bowing the whole way, Terrie approached the bed. But as she leaned over in another curtsy, Charlotte whacked her on the head with a pillow. The surprise of the blow knocked Terrie over. She immediately jumped up, grabbed a pillow and smacked Charlotte hard across the shoulders.

And just like that, they were in a pillow fight. Charlotte in Terrie's jeans had the advantage as they raced around the room hitting each other with every pillow they could find. Tiny down feathers blew everywhere like a miniature snow-

storm. They were both laughing so hard their stomachs hurt.

Suddenly Charlotte stopped laughing and put her finger to her lips. "Hush."

Alarmed by Charlotte's expression, Terrie stopped in mid-swing. In the instant silence, she heard voices from downstairs. One of them was a man's.

"That is Grandpapa. They must have returned early." Charlotte looked pale.

If only I could faint, Terrie prayed, or disappear, or go up in smoke. Grandpapa is the king and I'm in the queen's bedroom. She raced for the door, stopped, then ran back into the room to try to straighten it up. She had no idea what she was doing.

Charlotte was cooler. She grabbed Terrie's arm. "Follow me."

On tiptoe, Charlotte led the way out of the queen's room. Now the voices were louder, as if everyone were right in the hall at the foot of the stairs. In her terror, Terrie tripped on her unfamiliar long skirts and almost fell. Only Charlotte's grip on her arm kept her on her feet. Charlotte opened a door at the end of the hall.

"Go down these stairs, through the kitchen, and take the door to your right into the wine cellar," Charlotte whispered. "From there you can get out into the garden."

A thousand questions ran through Terrie's mind. What if someone saw her? What if she took the wrong turn? What if Cook were in the kitchen? How would she get her clothes back? There wasn't time to ask any of them. She had to hurry. In her bare feet, she ran down the twisting back stairs. Cautiously she pulled the kitchen door open. She didn't see or hear anyone. With her heart beating double-quick time, she ran across the cold brick floor to the door on her right. Narrow little stairs led down into the wine cellar. The underground room was dark and damp, but a chink of light ahead showed the way. Terrie raced across the hard dirt floor picking her way between the rows of wine bottles and stacked-up kegs. And then she was pushing against the outside cellar doors. Bright daylight greeted her. Wonderful, wonderful daylight.

As Terrie paused to catch her breath, she heard a soft whistle above her. She looked up. Charlotte was leaning out her third-floor bedroom window with a bundle in her arms. She dropped it. Terrie leaped back as it came sailing through the air and landed with a thud at her feet. It was her sweater and jeans and sneakers all neatly tied up. Terrie had to laugh. Charlotte was too much. In fact, this time, Charlotte had been a little *too* much. It had been a morning to remember.

CHAPTER   7

For the next couple of weeks, Terrie and Charlotte and Lioni met almost every day. Whether or not they got together all depended on Lioni. If Terrie found Lioni, or rather if Lioni found Terrie, he would lead her to Charlotte. Without Lioni, Terrie could never find Charlotte on her own.

It was hard for Terrie to keep the secret from her parents. They knew something was up. They both noticed her good mood and questioned her about it. She finally told them she had a new friend named Charlie. They were delighted. Mrs. Wright packed snacks for them. Mr. Wright said he would treat them to a movie. They wanted to meet her. No, Charlie wasn't there every day. Terrie never knew when she'd come and when she wouldn't. Terrie stalled and ducked and tried not to lie. And they accepted it, happy that she was happy.

On Tuesdays, Terrie and Charlotte always met in their rhododendron hideout by the Queen's

Cottage. They had named it Maze House and marked off rooms in the dirt, the state apartments, the throne room, the drawing room, the bedchambers. The thick branches were perfect for climbing and sitting and playing and Charlotte had even brought out rugs and cushions to make Maze House more comfortable.

The last Tuesday in July was a perfect day to play and Lioni led Terrie right into Maze House. The sun dappled through the dark leaves making sunny patterns underfoot. Terrie had brought a new game of Chinese checkers for them to play. But as she crawled in their secret back entrance, she heard crying.

Terrie was amazed. She had known Charlotte to be happy or angry or silly or stuck-up, but she had never known Charlotte to cry.

"What happened, Charlotte?"

Charlotte quickly turned her back. "Nothing."

"What's wrong? Tell me."

"No."

"Are you sick?" Terrie asked.

"I'm never sick."

"Then what is it?"

Charlotte turned around. She must have been crying a long time. Her eyes were red and her face was blotchy. "I haven't seen my mother all summer. Now she wants to visit with me. Grandpapa says yes but Papa says no. They had a terrible fight. Papa has left and Grandpapa has taken to bed. Now my grandmother's word is final and she has forbidden me to see Mama."

Charlotte was crying again. "Mama has sent word she will come up the River Thames Thursday next and that I am to meet her. If only I could. But it's impossible. Grandmama is watching me like a hawk and hardly lets me out of her sight."

Terrie thought about her own mother and father. She saw them every day and just accepted it. She couldn't imagine what it would be like not to have them around. Together.

"That's terrible, Charlotte," she said. "It must be against the law or illegal or something not to be able to see your own mother."

Charlotte laughed through her tears. "There aren't any rules when you're the queen. Grandmama can do anything she pleases."

Granny had wanted Terrie to visit for the summer and Terrie had wanted to go more than anything in the world. But her parents had said no. Terrie had been angry a long time, but to tell the truth, she hadn't thought about Granny or Cape Cod for weeks.

Charlotte wiped her eyes on the hem of her dress. "It vexes me too much to talk about it. Here, show me your new game before Miss Hayman orders me in."

Terrie had a hard time keeping her mind on Chinese checkers. It wasn't fair that someone's grandmother could tell a person what to do or not to do. Charlotte was forbidden to see her own mother. It was . . . it was the pits, that's what it was.

Charlotte couldn't stay long. As she gathered her things together, Terrie studied her, really studied her, from head to toe. She and Charlotte looked a lot alike, though Charlotte was a little taller and thinner. And their hair was exactly the same blonde color. After Charlotte left, Terrie packed up her Chinese checkers. But her mind wasn't on Chinese checkers. It was on Charlotte . . . and herself.

CHAPTER 8

"You want your hair cut? I don't believe it." Mrs. Wright stopped in the middle of pouring juice. Even Mr. Wright looked up from his morning paper.

"It's no big deal. I'm tired of long hair, that's all. I'd like it cut to about here." Terrie ran her finger along the back of her neck.

"That short? How about just taking off two or three inches?"

"No, Mom. If it can't be really short, I don't want it cut at all." That was a risk, but Terrie had to take it.

"Since I've been nagging you about your hair for months, I certainly won't argue about a few inches. In fact, Terrie, let's get it done today before you change your mind."

It was hard not to cry when the barber started cutting. Great snippets of hair lay on the floor like a blonde shag rug. Even Mom looked a little shaken. But Terrie had to go through with it. She shut her eyes and didn't watch.

Charlotte was surprised at Terrie's decision, too. "At last you've done something about your ridiculous American hair. Now you must do something about your ridiculous American name."

It was one of Charlotte's Princess-Charlotte-Augusta-future-queen-of-England days. In fact, she was so impossible, Terrie didn't even feel like talking about her plan. Then in the middle of a game of backgammon, Charlotte's eyes filled with tears.

"Grandmama is keeping a tighter watch on me than ever. Oh, Terrie, I just know I'll never get away to meet Mama on Thursday."

Of course Terrie had to tell Charlotte her plan. Charlotte was acting impossible because she was too upset to act any other way.

"Listen Charlotte, I've been thinking about something . . ." Terrie began and though no one was about, she leaned close to Charlotte and whispered. "First of all," she began, "we'll meet as usual on Thursday . . ."

How slowly the days passed. It seemed as if Thursday would never come. Then at last it arrived. As soon as Terrie woke up, she looked out her bedroom window. It was a gray day, overcast, with clouds. If only it didn't rain. Rain would ruin everything.

Terrie had never known her mother to be so

slow getting started in the morning. First she dusted, which she almost never did, then she ran two loads of wash. She puttered around for what seemed like forever. At last they were on their way. As soon as they were through the main gate, Terrie took off. Her tote bag bumped against her legs as she ran around to the side entrance of Kew Palace garden. She opened the gate, rushed through, then stopped. She had never seen the garden so crowded. All sorts of people wandered around. A photographer was taking pictures from the back palace steps. Two gardeners had turned off the fountain and were working on it. Some woman was lecturing to a group of ladies by the herb garden.

Terrie closed her eyes and wished everyone

away. Gone, begone with you. She wished so hard, when she opened her eyes she couldn't believe everyone was still there. Not only still there, but a troupe of about twenty Girl Guides in uniform was just coming around the corner talking and laughing.

Terrie had to be crazy. Charlotte, Lioni, her plan, were all something she had dreamed up. The summer had been so boring, her imagination had been working overtime. That was all there was to it. And here she had her hair cut for nothing. She scuffed her sneakers along the gravel path up to the gazebo and sank down on the bench.

She glanced out over the Thames. A houseboat was anchored on the opposite shore with a woman hanging up laundry on the deck. A power boat zoomed past. A barge full of sightseers chugged by. And she was expecting Charlotte's mother to come sailing up the Thames all secret and mysterious. She wasn't crazy, she was stupid.

"Woorf."

At first Terrie didn't register. Then she sat up straight. No dogs were allowed in the Kew Palace garden. Ever. That could only be one dog and that dog was Lioni. Terrie grabbed the bag of dog biscuits she'd packed in her tote bag and ran down the path in the direction of the barking. She was behind the holly hedge now, out of sight of Kew Palace and the rest of the garden.

"Woorf. Woorf."

The barking came from the far side of the garden by the north brick wall. Terrie scooted around a row of cherry trees and there was Lioni. And Charlotte. Terrie wasn't crazy after all, or even stupid.

"Oh, Charlotte, I'm so glad to see you," she cried.

But Charlotte, all dressed up in her shepherdess costume, looked worried. "I'm not sure I can go through with this, Terrie. It's a frightful crime to disobey the queen."

Frightful or not, Terrie wasn't about to give up now, not when she had thought everything was in her imagination then discovered it wasn't. "It will all work out fine, Charlotte. I know it will."

Before Charlotte could protest further, Terrie pulled off her sweater, unzipped her jeans and laid them on the bench for Charlotte. Reluctantly, Charlotte took off her silk shepherdess dress and petticoats and handed them to Terrie along with her lace picture hat and, most important of all, her mask. Terrie put on the petticoats first, then the gown, while Charlotte dressed in Terrie's clothes. This time Charlotte knew what to do with the zipper. There, they were done. Each wore the other's clothing. Lioni must have sensed their excitement. He barked and ran back and forth between them.

Charlotte gave Terrie a little push toward the garden. "Hurry, if you don't appear soon, Miss Hayman will come searching."

Terrie fluffed up her hair to look more like Charlotte's and started for the garden with Lioni on his leash. There wasn't time to see if Charlotte made it safely over the wall. They had set up a wooden bench under a cherry tree. Charlotte was to climb from the bench into the tree, and from there over the wall. Once on the other side, it was only a short distance to the riverbank where her mother would be waiting.

In the meantime, Terrie was to take Charlotte's place in the Kew Palace garden. As she rounded the corner with Lioni, she was startled to see the fountain working and the garden empty. Of course it was empty. It wouldn't be filled with Girl Guides and photographers and Garden Club ladies in the year 1805. Only the weather was the same, cloudy and overcast with the threat of rain.

Careful to keep the mask up to her face, Terrie walked over to the fountain, sat down on the bench, tied Lioni's leash to one of its legs, and picked up the writing kit Charlotte had left for her. Charlotte had told Miss Hayman she wanted to wear her shepherdess costume this morning to make certain it fit, and promised to sit quietly and write a few letters. Terrie opened the ink pot,

dipped in the quill pen and started to write. But her hand was shaking too much to do anything but scribble.

Whew, Charlotte's dress was tight. What if Terrie ripped it? And what if someone came out into the garden and spoke to her? She could cover her face with the mask, but her American accent would give her away. All of a sudden, Terrie panicked. She was sure to be found out. Charlotte was worried about getting in trouble. At least Charlotte was a princess. Terrie was a nobody and nobodies used to get beheaded all the time in England. It was a terrible thought. It might happen to her. She would disappear forever and no one would ever know what had become of her.

CHAPTER   9

"Princess Charlotte!"

Terrie almost jumped off the bench. It was Miss Hayman's clear and commanding voice calling from an upstairs palace window. Terrie forced herself not to turn around as she waved her hand to show that she had heard.

"Princess Charlotte, have you forgotten the king's morning musicale? Please come in directly."

Terrie froze. She couldn't move. She couldn't even swallow. A musicale. In her excitement, Charlotte must have forgotten it. What could she do? Where could she go? Terrie's mind raced in a dozen directions and came up with a blank.

"Princess Charlotte, don't delay any longer."

Now Miss Hayman sounded angry. Terrie had to do something, but she didn't know what. If she stayed here in the garden, Miss Hayman would come out. If she tried to run away, they were sure to catch her. Either way, she would be found out.

All she could do was go into the palace and hope for the best. At least she had her mask. Holding it to her face with one hand, Terrie scooped up Lioni with the other, gave him a dog biscuit to keep him happy and headed for the palace. Though she was certain Miss Hayman was watching from the upstairs window, she didn't dare look. Luckily Charlotte's too-long skirts hid her sneakers.

Terrie climbed the back palace stairs as slowly as if she were mounting the executioner's block. Which might well be what she was doing, she realized with a jolt. Breathless with fear, she opened the palace door and stepped into the back hall. To her right she knew was the kitchen and servants' wing and to her left was the King's Breakfast Room. Straight ahead was the front hall and staircase leading to the second floor.

"Princess Charlotte, Her Majesty your grandmother has requested that you change out of your shepherdess gown before the musicale begins." It was Miss Hayman's voice coming down the stairs. "Your aunts and uncles have just arrived . . ."

Now Terrie could see Miss Hayman's long skirts descend the staircase. In a moment they would be face to face. Terrie had to get out of here. She raced for the King's Breakfast Room, slipped inside, and closed the door quietly behind her. The empty room was lined with rows of gold cane chairs with a harpsichord set at the far end. This must be where the musicale was to be held.

With Lioni still clutched in her arms, Terrie ran the length of the room to the door at the opposite end. But just as she was about to turn the knob, she heard voices on the other side. Lots and lots of voices. The aunts and uncles must be gathering for the musicale. She was trapped.

Dungeons. Chains. Torture. Bread and water. All sorts of images flashed through Terrie's mind. In a complete panic, she surveyed the room. There were no closets to hide in and the curtains were too thin to conceal her. But what about those window seats? If they were like the window seats in Terrie's house back home, they opened for use as storage.

Lioni whimpered and whined in Terrie's arms. She had to keep him still. Quickly she fed him another dog biscuit and ran across the room, thankful for her silent sneakers. Yes, the window seats had pull latches that lifted up.

"Have you seen Princess Charlotte, Lieutenant?"

It was Miss Hayman right outside the door. Terrie didn't even give herself time to think. She just yanked open the window seat and jumped inside with Lioni. Carefully she lowered the lid. But there was no air. She wedged her mask under the lid to get an inch or two of breathing space.

Lioni was terrified. He cried and squirmed to get out. Terrie reached into her bag for another biscuit. There were only two left. But that was terrible. Without his dog biscuits to keep him quiet, Lioni was sure to act up and give them both away.

Terrie squinted out the air space. People were filing into the room. Chairs scraped on the floor as everyone took their places. At least their backs were to the window seat and they were making enough noise to cover up the sound of Lioni's crunching. Then without warning, the room was silent, completely silent. A few notes tinkled on the harpsichord. Now that he had finished his biscuit, Lioni was whimpering again. Terrie was almost whimpering herself. There was only one biscuit left. Just as she was about to feed it to Lioni, from out of nowhere, she had an idea. She didn't know whether it would work or not, but she had to try it.

Slowly, carefully, Terrie opened the window
seat. She waved the last biscuit under Lioni's nose
to tempt him, then tossed it out into the middle
of the room. In one quick motion, she half lowered, half threw Lioni out after it. He sailed
through the air and landed on the bare floor, slid-
ing and yelping as he tried to regain his balance.
And then he was on his feet chasing his biscuit.

All the guests jumped up as a barking Lioni
darted and skidded under and around their chairs.

The room was in an uproar. Ladies screamed. Men shouted. It was now or never for Terrie. As soon as everyone realized it was only Lioni, the confusion would be over. She threw back the window seat cover, jumped out and ran for the door. But as soon as she reached the back hall, she saw through the window that someone was standing right outside on the palace porch. It was a guard and he had a sword. And she had left her mask behind in the window seat. She was *still* trapped.

No, wait, there was the wine cellar that led out into the garden. It was her only chance. But when Terrie opened the kitchen door, she heard a voice humming inside. It must be Cook. Terrie peeked around the door. Cook was working at a table right in the middle of the kitchen. There was no way Terrie could get past her without being seen. Then Cook picked up two pans from the table and carried them over to the big brick oven

by the wall. With her back to Terrie, she bent over the open oven door.

Terrie took a deep breath, held up her long silk skirts and ran across the kitchen floor faster than she had ever run before. She eased open the wine cellar door and hurried down the stairs. Then she was in the wine cellar, dodging around the kegs and barrels and racks of bottles in the dim light. She thrust the heavy doors open. She was outside. And safe. Now all she had to do was meet Charlotte.

Sticking close to the shadows of the high brick wall, Terrie ran around to the north end of the garden. Charlotte was waiting for her.

"Listen, Charlotte," Terrie tried to explain as she peeled off Charlotte's clothes and put on her own, "you might find sort of a mess inside the Palace. You see, Lioni . . ."

But Charlotte didn't let her finish. "Oh Terrie, it was so wonderful to see Mama. We had such a

lovely visit. Now I have seen Mama I know I can get through the rest of the summer and endure what has to be endured."

"I'm glad it worked out, Charlotte, but . . . but . . ." Terrie couldn't possibly explain what had happened to her.

Apparently Charlotte didn't care. She slipped into her shepherdess gown, then leaned over and gave Terrie a quick hug. "You are my true friend. There is no way I can thank you." And before Terrie could even reply, she was gone.

CHAPTER 10

Terrie couldn't wait to see Charlotte the next day to hear what happened when Charlotte went back into the palace. But though Terrie looked everywhere for Charlotte and Lioni, she didn't find them. Maybe they were being punished for ruining the king's musicale. Even when Terrie didn't find them the following Monday, she didn't worry. She was sure to find them the next day out by Maze House where they always met on Tuesdays.

Tuesday was warm and sunny. Terrie walked out to the Queen's Cottage past the pond. It was out of her way but she wanted to see what the kids with the sailboats were up to. They were all there. The red-headed girl even called hello and waved her over. Terrie almost stopped. They looked like they were having fun, and someone had a big new boat that seemed to be the pride of the fleet. But she couldn't stay. She had to meet Charlotte.

Though Terrie searched from one end of Maze

House to the other, she didn't find either Lioni or Charlotte. In fact, she didn't see a footprint, a broken twig or any evidence of all the hours they had spent there. Terrie crawled out the secret back entrance. After a weekend of rain, the warm sun felt good. She lay on her back with her face to the sky, wondering what to do next.

"Woorf."

Terrie was on her feet in a second. It was Lioni running across the grass. His ears flew back and his pink tongue hung out. Terrie took off after him. But that was strange. Instead of leading Terrie into Maze House, he was headed in the opposite direction. He was, in fact, headed right for an old man sitting on a bench. The old man clapped his hands and called to him.

"Scooter, you naughty boy. Where have you been?"

Lioni ran toward the old man who reached out and grabbed him. The man noticed Terrie watching. "Poor old Scooter and me would get in terrible trouble if anyone saw him. Dogs are against park rules. You won't tell, will you?"

Scooter? Terrie stared as Lioni flopped down beside the bench. Only it wasn't Lioni. This dog was bigger and much older. No, it wasn't Lioni at all.

Terrie was too surprised to answer. She had been so sure the dog was Lioni and Lioni would lead her

to Charlotte the way he always did. Suddenly she realized something. She wouldn't see Charlotte or Lioni again. Not ever. When Charlotte had said she could get through the rest of the summer once she saw her mother, she was saying good-bye. They weren't meant to meet again. Then Terrie realized something else. They didn't have to. Each of them had helped the other when she needed it most. Terrie knew now she could get through the rest of the summer, too.

Terrie rubbed her arms to warm them. The sun was still out, but a brisk breeze had come up. Actually it was just the right kind of breeze for sailing boats. Maybe those kids at the pond would let her play with them if she asked. And hadn't Dad promised to buy her a sailboat? Terrie took one last long look at the dark thicket of Maze House and turned away. She heard the white dog give a friendly bark, but she didn't look back. She just picked up her pace and began to run. Now that she knew where she was going, she couldn't wait to get there.

AUTHOR'S NOTE

Princess Charlotte Augusta was born in 1796 and died in 1817 at the age of twenty-one. Princess Charlotte, the only child of King George IV, was greatly loved, and all of England mourned her passing. Had she lived, she would have been crowned queen of England in 1830 at the time of her father's death.